Nour's SECRET LIBRARY

WRITTEN BY Wafa' Tarnowska

ILLUSTRATED BY Vali Mintzi

Barefoot Books
Step inside a story

There was a girl named Nour who lived in the city of Damascus, which was described by those who loved it as the "fragrant place." Apricot and cherry orchards surrounded it like a sweet-scented belt, while rose perfume filled its streets. But one day, the city began to lose its fragrance, because war was knocking at its gates with its smelly tanks and noisy guns.

Nour's name means "light" in Arabic. It was indeed perfect for a girl whose face was as round as the moon, whose eyes were as bright as stars and who brought joy to everyone she knew.

The person Nour loved most in the world, after her Mama and Baba, was her cousin Amir, who was like a brother to her. When they finished their schoolwork, Nour and Amir would climb trees, play hide-and-seek and jump over puddles. They especially loved reading adventure stories about detectives. They wished they could find treasures and go camping, have picnics and solve mysteries like the characters in the books. They dreamed most of all about having their own secret society — a club just for their friends.

Nour and Amir looked for a meeting place for their secret society down the winding alleys of their ancient city. They decided who should be invited, and even invented a secret handshake.

After months of planning, they were ready. The Secret Society of the Damascus Seven would meet in the storeroom of Baba's bakery. The invitations went out to five carefully chosen friends along with a secret password. Baba promised to bake his famous yellow saffron cake covered with almonds for the occasion.

The morning of their first meeting, Nour woke up to the sound of planes circling overhead. Moments later, shells exploded, shaking their windowpanes.

"What's happening?" cried Nour.

"I think the fighting we've seen nearby has spread to our part of town," Mama said, watching the sky through the window. "We need to stay inside and wait for the fighting to stop."

"When will it stop?" asked Nour.

"When people talk and try to work out their differences," answered Baba.

"Will that happen today?" asked Nour, thinking of the secret society password she'd stayed up late to memorize.

"No," said Mama. "Not today. In the meantime, we need to keep safe in Umm Ali's basement."

The basement was dark and damp, with only one small barred window at street level. Thirty people huddled in a space designed for six. When the electricity was cut, people read books and newspapers by flashlight or candlelight. The grown-ups listened to the news on their phones while the children played cards at their feet.

Everyone hid in their
basements at night during
the worst of the fighting.
The soldiers often rested in the
daytime, which gave people a short
and precious chance to go home or out
for supplies. The souk was shut down and
there was very little fresh food, and certainly
no sweets, biscuits or treats. At first, Nour's Baba
brought over some leftover pastries from the bakery,
which he carried down to the basement with hot, sweet
tea. But after a while, bread was only available once a day,
and Nour and her family often went to sleep hungry.

The fighting lasted for days on end. Nour and the other children stayed safe in their buildings' basements at night. They could not play outside anymore. All of the schools closed. So did all the shops. Playgrounds emptied and birds disappeared. Streets turned into dangerous battlefields. Some young people joined the fight. Others hid at home waiting for the fighting to end and for schools to open again.

But they had to wait a long time, because buildings around them were shelled one by one. They collapsed into huge piles of rubble, spilling the things inside onto the streets like open suitcases.

Whenever there was a lull in the fighting, Amir was sent out to buy bread. On his way to his uncle's bakery, he started picking up books he found in the streets. He brought them home and divided them into dusty piles according to subjects. When he told his friends about it, they started picking up books too while they were out to buy supplies.

"What are you going to do with all these books?" asked Nour. "Your bedroom is full of them, and they're spilling everywhere into the hall and dining room."

"My friends and I started collecting them," he answered. "But I don't know what to do with them all."

"Why don't we create a secret library?" Nour whispered. "We could start a reading club for everyone."

"That's a great idea!" cried Amir.

"Shhh!" Nour looked around. "The first thing we need is a secret location."

"Is this our new secret then?" Amir whispered.

Nour smiled. "It's our new secret."

First, Nour and Amir cleaned the dusty books. Nour was amazed by the stacks of volumes Amir and his friends found in the rubble, each one different. Every book was like a person wanting to be loved, with a unique personality and soul.

It felt safe and wonderful to be surrounded by books from floor to ceiling: big books, small books, thin books and fat books. Some were in Arabic, while others were in foreign languages — English, Armenian, Greek, French, even Hebrew and Syriac.

The world of books is wonderful,
Nour thought, looking at the piles of
books around her. *Like a galaxy full of
stars. Some are shinier than others, but
together they make the sky sparkle.*

Amir and Nour found an empty basement
in a half-destroyed building. A couple of families
lived in the floors above, but everyone else had fled.
With the help of their friends, they transported the books
one backpack at a time to their secret location. It took such
courage to walk slowly carrying the heavy loads, with the risk
of bullets whizzing past. They were lucky that no one was injured.

Whenever there was a lull in the shelling, Nour, Amir and their friends would sneak into their new library and build shelves with planks of wood they found in the rubble. If they found a table or a cushion or a chair, they would bring them down too.

They named the library Al-Fajr, which means "dawn" in Arabic, because they hoped for a new dawn after so many dark nights.

The library opened every single day from morning to dark. It only closed for the Friday prayer. Rescuers borrowed medical books to learn about the human body and how to treat wounds. Teachers looked for ideas for home lessons. Even Nour's Baba borrowed cookbooks to learn how to make foreign pastries and cakes, looking forward to a day when he could once again try out new recipes.

One boy called Amjad visited the library every day. He lived next door, and it was safer for him to stay in a basement rather than above ground — and more fun to spend the day reading. He loved the library so much that Nour and Amir found him a desk and chair and appointed him deputy librarian. They even taught him the secret handshake.

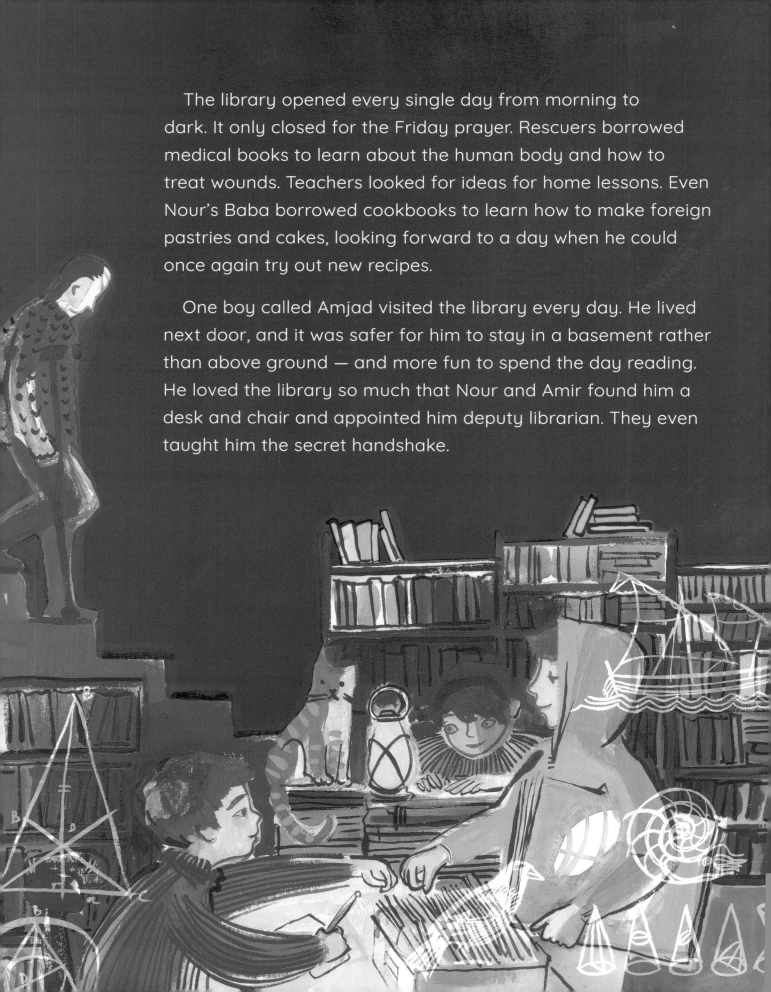

As word of the secret library spread, more people helped gather books. From backpack to backpack and carload to carload, the library grew and flourished. It grew to thousands of books, all gathered from abandoned apartments by brave volunteers.

"Well done, my darling," said Baba to Nour. "Your library has become a shining light. I am so proud of you and Amir!" He gave them both a big hug. "Girls and boys, young and old, soldiers and civilians . . . What is it about the books that brings them all here?"

Nour sighed. "I guess reading keeps everyone's minds busy," she said. "Books don't fight with each other like people do."

For years, Nour and Amir's hidden
library remained the best-kept secret in town. The
children talked to their books and their books listened to them.
Their secret library had become a safe port in a sea of war. The hope it
brought carried them from the darkness of destruction into a bright new dawn.

About SYRIA

Syria's capital, Damascus, is one of the oldest cities in the world. It is called Al-Sham in Arabic.

The Umayyad Mosque in Damascus is considered the fourth holiest site in Islam. It is located next to the famous Hamidiyah Souk, which sells clothes, handicrafts, fabrics, spices, candied fruit and delicious ice cream!

The Syrian city of Aleppo is famous for its pistachio nuts and laurel soaps, which help improve skin conditions. Roses from Damascus are used for perfumes and jams, and a beautiful cloth called damask is named after the city.

Syria's national flower is jasmine, and its national tree is the olive tree. Date palms grow by the Euphrates River. Fruit trees such as almonds, apricots, plums and pomegranates grow by the Barada River. Syria also grows cotton and spices.

The Syrian Desert, called Badiyat Al-Sham in Arabic, is the tenth largest desert in the world. It extends beyond Syria into Jordan, Saudi Arabia and Iraq. It is home to snakes, lizards, gazelles and jerboas (jumping desert rodents that can run 24 km — about 15 miles — per hour!).

Arabic is the official language of Syria, but Kurdish, Armenian, Hebrew and Syriac are also spoken. The majority of Syrians are Muslims (87%), living alongside Christian and Jewish minorities.

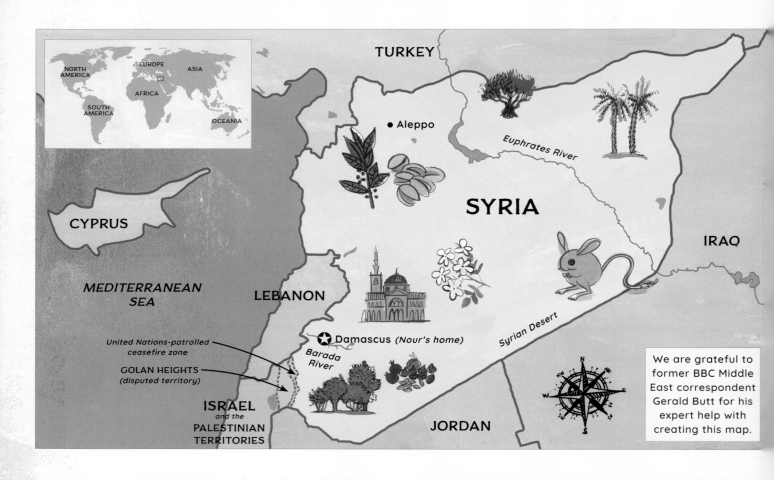

We are grateful to former BBC Middle East correspondent Gerald Butt for his expert help with creating this map.

GLOSSARY

Amir: personal name meaning "prince" (Arabic)

Baba: Dad (Arabic)

The Friday Prayer: Muslims' community prayer held in mosques at midday, called Salat al-Jumu'ah in Arabic

shell: a container filled with explosives that is sent flying through the air as a weapon

souk: market (Arabic)

Umm: mother (Arabic). "Umm Ali" means "mother of Ali." A respectful way of addressing people who are parents in Arabic

This book uses the abbreviations **BCE** and **CE** to describe dates in history. They stand for "before common era" and "common era." You might have also heard of the terms **BC** and **AD**, which stand for the Latin words that mean "before the birth of Jesus Christ" and "after the death of Jesus Christ." The "common era" is also measured before and after this event.

8 FAMOUS LIBRARIES
of the Middle East

7th century BCE: The library of King Ashurbanipal in Nineveh, the world's largest city at the time, held clay tablets of two of the world's most ancient stories: the Epic of Creation and the Epic of Gilgamesh.

7th century BCE: The libraries of King Nebuchadnezzar II in Babylon helped the city become a hub for arts and learning.

3rd century BCE: The Great Library of Alexandria in Egypt held thousands of scrolls. It was part of a larger research institution called the "Mouseion" dedicated to the Muses, the nine goddesses of the arts.

1200 BCE: The Libraries of Ugarit, located in modern-day Syria, held the Baal Cycle Tablets, which were the epic poems of the Canaanites.

221 BCE: The Royal Library of Antioch in Ancient Syria was commissioned by Antiochus the Great, a successor to Alexander the Great. It became a hub of research and philosophy.

4th century CE: The Imperial Library of Constantinople (now Istanbul) preserved the knowledge of the ancient Greeks and Romans for almost 1,000 years.

8th century CE: The House of Wisdom in Baghdad, founded by the Caliph Harun al-Rashid, housed his many manuscripts, welcomed scientific research and opened a translation department, where books in Greek, Latin, Persian and Sanskrit were translated into Arabic.

1005 CE: The House of Wisdom in Cairo held over 100,000 volumes. The medieval historian Ibn Abi Tayyi described it as a "Wonder of the World."

THE *Real* SECRET LIBRARY

This story was inspired by young people living in the town of Daraya southwest of Damascus. At the beginning of the Syrian civil war in 2011, the government cut off Daraya's water, electricity and food supplies. For four years, the town was attacked and damaged. While many of Daraya's residents fled, about 8,000 people stayed. Despite the terror above ground, Daraya's young people saved 15,000 books from bombed-out houses and created a library in the basement of an abandoned building. When this book was printed, the war in Syria was still ongoing.

CULTURE *and* WAR

Throughout history, many libraries, ancient valuables and historical sites have been destroyed by war. When the House of Wisdom and Baghdad's other 36 public libraries were destroyed by the Mongols in 1258 CE, the Tigris and Euphrates rivers became black with ink. The Mongols threw the books in the water and used their leather covers to make sandals. Precious knowledge was lost forever.

For a library to be built during a war is unique and miraculous. As the co-director of the secret library of Daraya, Abu el-Ezz, said, "Books are our way to wipe out ignorance." When we read, we see the world through others' eyes. Our differences seem smaller, and the divisions that lead to war can break down.

AUTHOR'S Note

This story is inspired by a true event during the Syrian war, but it is also based on my experiences during the civil war in Lebanon in 1975–76. I found myself hiding in a basement for several months with my family to stay safe from bombs. All twelve families from our building spent every night in the caretaker's basement. Forty children and adults played card games, drank coffee, shared food, listened to the radio and tried to make jokes despite the horrors happening outside.

I never wanted to share these memories until I read the story of the secret library of Daraya. It reminded me of how I also took refuge in books during the endless shelling at night. We had no electricity, so I used my flashlight to devour one book after another.

To escape, I read the most difficult books I could find. I read about people who were suffering more than I was. Those books gave me courage to cope with the senseless destruction happening around me.

Books are one of the ways people cope with disaster, war and despair. "Books are like rain," said one of the Daraya librarians. "Whenever rain falls, things grow." I believe that our souls need books just like our bodies need food. I hope that reading this book has fed your soul, for writing it has fed mine.

— Wafa' Tarnowska

ILLUSTRATOR'S Note

I feel very connected to Nour's story. Looking back at my childhood in communist Romania, I remember living in fear, and using art and books (preferably those with pictures!) to escape reality. Since then, for the past 30 years, I have lived in the Middle East. Like Nour and Amir, I sometimes feel the deep conflict between war and peace present in everyday life.

To create the illustrations for this book I studied many pictures depicting the people and places of Damascus. I found it very moving and sad to see so many images of the beautiful, ancient city before the war alongside the images of devastation the war has caused.

When I began to draw sketches in my notebook, I realized that the most difficult challenge would be communicating the realities of war while also giving a sense of life and hope. With this in mind, I decided to work in two different styles. I used charcoal for the rough and ruined landscapes of the city, and thick, vibrant gouache for the bright, hopeful story of the children and the library.

It was a very meaningful experience working on a story about children surviving war with Lebanese-born writer Wafa' Tarnowska. There aren't many opportunities to illustrate such challenging stories, and I find it amazing that even in times of fear and destruction, children's imaginations can keep the human spirit alive.

— Vali Mintzi

Grateful thanks to Amro Arida for his help with bringing this book to life.

Barefoot Books • 23 Bradford Street, 2nd Floor • Concord, MA 01742
Barefoot Books • 29/30 Fitzroy Square • London, W1T 6LQ

Text copyright © 2022 by Wafa' Tarnowska
Illustrations copyright © 2022 by Vali Mintzi
The moral rights of Wafa' Tarnowska and Vali Mintzi have been asserted

First published in the United States of America by Barefoot Books, Inc and in Great Britain by Barefoot Books, Ltd in 2022. All rights reserved

Graphic design by Sarah Soldano, Barefoot Books
Edited and art directed by Kate DePalma, Barefoot Books
Educational notes by Wafa' Tarnowska and Autumn Allen
Reproduction by Bright Arts, Hong Kong. Printed in Malaysia
This book was typeset in Caprizant, Charcuterie, Mr Lucky and Quicksand
The illustrations were prepared in pencil, gouache and charcoal

Hardback ISBN 978-1-64686-291-7 • Paperback ISBN 978-1-64686-292-4
E-book ISBN 978-1-64686-349-5

British Cataloguing-in-Publication Data: a catalogue record for this book is available from the British Library

Library of Congress Cataloging-in-Publication Data is available under LCCN 2021947208

1 3 5 7 9 8 6 4 2